"With all of Simon James Green's si[...] both Alfie and Harvey learn that the [...] to live up to are their own – an impo[...]
IRISH EXAMINER

"Delightfully funny, uplifting and swee[...] promposal drama I wish I'd had as a teen" **WREN JAMES**

"*The Big Ask* tells the hilariously heartwarming story of two boys and their foray into romance and bravery … [Simon's] stories always remind me of why I love YA so much" **FARIDAH ÀBÍKÉ-ÍYÍMÍDÉ**

"Fizzes with joy, wit and hope" **IAN EAGLETON**

"I was unable to keep the cheesiest grin off my face reading *The Big Ask* … Full of Simon's trademark wit and hilarity, *The Big Ask* is utterly gorgeous! There's no other word for it" **GEORGE LESTER**

"I loved this charming, funny and incredibly sweet read … Set in the run-up to prom night, it's packed with Simon's trademark wit, emotion and chaos" **LISA WILLIAMSON**

"Accessible, smart and immensely relatable, it resonates with those real teenage anxieties of labelling who we are" **DAVID FENNE**

"Absolutely gorgeous characters and a great story about being yourself and finding people that love you for who you are and not who they want you to be" **CAROLINE FIELDING, YLG COMMITTEE**

"A funny, relatable queer promposal story you'll read at a sitting. Packed full of heart and hopeful with it" **NE BOOK AWARDS**

"Funny, kind and hopeful … Schools – this is perfect to have in the library for all those kids who have a prom coming up"
NEXT PAGE BOOKS

"Perfect for *Heartstopper* fans … authentic and relatable for all readers … Joyful, sensitive and heartwarming, *The Big Ask* will give you the warm, fuzzy feelings of a first love without labels"
CHECK 'EM OUT BOOKS

The Big Ask

SIMON JAMES GREEN

Barrington Stoke

Published by Barrington Stoke
An imprint of HarperCollins*Publishers*
Westerhill Road, Bishopbriggs, Glasgow, G64 2QT

www.barringtonstoke.co.uk

HarperCollins*Publishers*
Macken House, 39/40 Mayor Street Upper,
Dublin 1, DO1 C9W8, Ireland

First published in 2024

ISBN 978-1-80090-242-8

10 9 8 7 6 5 4 3 2

Printed and Bound in the UK using 100% Renewable Electricity
at Martins the Printers Ltd

MIX
Paper | Supporting
responsible forestry
FSC
www.fsc.org
FSC™ C007454

This book contains FSC™ certified paper and other controlled
sources to ensure responsible forest management.

For more information visit: www.harpercollins.co.uk/green

For everyone out there with questions.
Take your time. You'll work it out.

CHAPTER 1

FOUR DAYS TO PROM

"Epic news, right?!" Jasminder says.

She's grinning at me, her eyes wide, hardly able to contain her excitement at whatever the news is.

I'd assumed that the urgent hammering at the door was my McDonald's delivery. Obviously I didn't want to miss *that*, which is why I shot straight downstairs. And which is why I'm standing here in just my T-shirt and boxers.

"What's happened?" I mutter.

Jas squints at me. "You haven't heard?" she says. "Seriously, Alfie? You haven't heard? It's all over social media!"

I shrug. "Is someone dead?" I ask.

"It's bigger than that," Jas replies, pushing past me into the hall. "This is … *a revolution*."

I shut the front door and wipe the sleep from my eyes. (OK, I *may* have dozed off after ordering McDonald's on my phone and, yeah, it's noon, but don't judge me.) I follow Jas into the lounge, where's she's pacing about in front of the fireplace.

She watches me flop down on the sofa and scowls. "Why aren't you dressed?" Jas asks. "It's, like, midday."

"I was up late," I say.

"Doing *what*? Exams finished last week."

I shrug because the truth is I went down a rabbit hole of videos featuring posh kids trying to rap. It was utterly cringe, but I couldn't look away … apparently for three hours.

Jas shakes her head like I'm an eternal disappointment. It's all right for her – she's standing in my living room wearing actual clothes and smelling all fragrant, like a normal human. Jas has her shit together, you know?

Jas knows what she wants to do with her life (be a doctor), whereas I don't.

Jas has a range of interests that give her reasons to get up and make plans (orchestra, politics, *archery*). Whereas I have more limited hobbies (sleep, food, a bit of gaming) that mean I have no reason to leave my bed.

Jas has even asked someone to prom – Joe Chan, no less! Jas is confident and funny and had the guts to ask one of the hottest boys in our year to be her prom date. Joe said yes, because when you're Jasminder Cheema, life just seems to work out.

Whereas I am going by myself like the tragic little loner I am. But here's the thing: I've made my peace with that. I'm happy sitting back, watching the world get on with life. Who needs the stress of participating? Or even just working out what to wear in the mornings?

I sigh. "What's the news then?" I ask.

Jas smiles at me, her eyes twinkling. "Harvey Ledger and Summer Gray ..."

I roll my eyes. Harvey and Summer are the school's golden couple. They've literally got it all – the looks, popularity, money. I mean, you could easily hate them, except Harvey's actually really nice (by which I mean he's hot AF and I really fancy him – not that anyone knows that). Summer ... well, Summer's ghastly, but she's president of the prom committee, so we all kinda have to tolerate her.

Anyway, whatever this news is, it's probably some minor prom drama that Summer's blown out of proportion, because that girl *loves* drama.

I glance back at Jas, whose eyes are wide to the point of popping out. "They have split up!" she chirps.

I did not hear that right. "Huh?" I say.

"They've split up. Harvey and Summer have split up. They are no more. *Finito!* Their relationship is over. Ended." Jas leans towards me. "Do you understand?"

The news filters into my brain and none of it makes sense. "They can't have," I mumble.

"They have."

"They've been together since Year Eight!"

"And now they're not," Jas says.

I feel like the rug's been pulled from under me. Harvey and Summer were born within an hour of each other. They have been eternally bonded in everyone's minds ever since, like the main characters in a fantasy novel.

Their parents immediately became friends, of course. There are pictures of baby Harvey wearing a romper suit that says "Ladies Man" on it. Next to him is baby Summer wearing one reading "My Guy!" with an arrow pointing at three-week-old Harvey.

Their parents would refer to Harvey and Summer as "boyfriend and girlfriend" even at the birthday parties we had as little kids – the ones before "popularity" became a factor in getting an invite. By Year Eight, they were official.

The rest of us were flailing around in the grip of hormones, breaking voices and general awkwardness in Year Eight. Meanwhile, Harvey and Summer were a full-on couple, showing us what life could be like if we'd been luckier when the good genes had been handed out.

Summer and Harvey became the one constant in all our lives. Teachers came and went, parents got divorced, puberty happened ... But during all the changes, there'd always been Harvey and Summer. They were like royalty, gliding above it all – our romantic heroes.

"What are you thinking?" Jas asks.

I blow out a breath. "That they'll probably get back together?"

"Summer is *fuming*," Jas replies. "She's told everyone it's over and changed her social media profiles from 'taken' to 'single'."

My eyes widen. So it's serious? Prom's in four days. This isn't the time to be messing about with dates. It's a time to be organising outfits, getting haircuts, and waxing hair in sensitive places, just in case you get lucky.

More importantly, Harvey and Summer suddenly being single might send the school's social structure into meltdown. I know about ten lads in Year Eleven who would drop *everything* to take Summer to prom – including the poor girls those lads are meant to be going with.

"What are you thinking?" Jas asks again.

"What a mess, huh?" I say, blowing out another breath. "I guess that's change for you. What did Mrs Harper tell us at our last assembly?

'So much is going to change in the next few months!' Guess she was right!" I shake my head. "Scary. I'm not sure I like change."

"Well, sure," Jas replies. "But change can also be an *opportunity*."

"How come?" I say.

Jas lowers her voice. "Harvey is now single. He might want a date to the prom. And you, Alfie, could ask him."

"Why would I do that?" I say quickly. "It's not like I fancy him."

"Lies!" Jas trills. "You were far too fast to deny it!"

"I've never told you I fancy Harvey!" I protest.

Jas grins at me. "You don't need to *tell* me. It's obvious from the way your eyes go all big whenever you look at him, like a sort of pining puppy."

"I can't help what my eyes do!" I say.

"Remember that time he came over in Science to ask if he could borrow a ruler?" Jas says. "You were so flustered you dropped your entire pencil case all over the floor!"

I shrug. "So?"

"And then Harvey gave you the ruler back later, and you thought I didn't see, but I saw you *stroke* it. You *stroked* the ruler, Alfie."

"No," I say.

"And then you smelled it," Jas goes on. "And that's when I *knew*."

I laugh, despite being horrified she saw all that, obviously. "None of that matters, because he's not gay," I tell her.

"You don't know that."

"He's been going out with Summer for years!"

"So?" says Jas. "Maybe Harvey's been working out his sexuality? Maybe he's bi, or pan! I saw him order an oat-milk latte once."

"Maybe it was for someone else, not because he's LGBTQ+!"

"He walks fast."

"He plays football – he's an *athlete*," I say.

"Gay people walk fast."

"No we don't. Well, not always. OK, mainly we do, but I still think …" I groan, frustrated. "Harvey Ledger is not going to be my date to prom. Boys like Harvey Ledger do not date boys like me. Have you seen me?" I extend my scrawny arms and pull up my T-shirt, revealing my skinny, white, untoned body, no six-pack in sight. "I'm a wreck."

"A *tragic* wreck who stays in bed all day," Jas adds.

"There you go."

"So it's time to change that. You should ask Harvey. Ask him, else you'll never know."

I laugh again and say, "Sure, sure."

"Else one day, on your deathbed, you'll wonder: *What if?! What if I'd asked Harvey Ledger to the prom – would my life have been totally different?*"

I take a deep breath and shake my head. If I didn't know Jas better, I'd say she was high.

"I just want you to have a nice time at prom, Alfie," she says.

"I will."

"And what else did Mrs Harper tell us in that leavers' assembly?" Jas asks.

"Anyone smuggling alcohol into the prom will be asked to leave immediately," I say.

"Not that."

"Hiding alcohol in the toilet cisterns won't work either – we're wise to it?" I try again.

"She said, '*Shoot for the stars!*'" Jas has a wistful look in her eye as she sweeps her hands out in front of her. She turns back to me. "Alfie Parker, it's time for you to shoot for the stars. And who knows, maybe you'll—"

"Miss and fall flat on my face?"

"Do you want ..." Jas looks me up and down. "*This?*"

Oh my god, my best friend thinks I'm tragic. I mean, *I* think I'm tragic, but I don't expect other people to be quite so ... *obvious* that that's what they think too. Whatever happened to telling white lies?

"I just think you could have so much more," Jas says. "You're a nice guy. You *should* have a date to prom."

"Jas, if Harvey's suddenly single, half the year will have asked him by now," I point out.

She shakes her head. "Everyone's probably thinking that, so no one actually has. Nobody had asked Joe Chan before I did – everyone just assumed he'd have a date."

The doorbell rings.

"That'll be my Big Mac," I mutter, heaving myself up.

"It's not your Big Mac," Jas replies, giving me a wicked smile. "It's Harvey Ledger."

CHAPTER 2

It *is* Harvey Ledger at the door.

I know Jas said it would be, but why would I believe her? It's completely outlandish. Harvey has never been to my house before. He doesn't know where I live.

And yet …

Here he is.

Standing in my doorway.

I have ten million questions. Some of which are:

- What is Harvey doing here?
- How can one human be so attractive?
- Where is my Big Mac anyway?

"Hi, Alfie," Harvey says.

For a moment, I'm totally paralysed. It's his dark brown eyes and the way his blond hair falls perfectly over his forehead. Not to mention the fact he's only wearing grey joggers and a white T-shirt but he still manages to look *amazing* and basically like the fantasy boyfriend of my wildest dreams ... And he knows my name. *He knows my name.*

"Alfie?" Harvey says again. "You OK?"

"What? Y-yes!" I stutter. "All good. Hi. *Hey.* What can I ...? Why are you ...? Sorry, I thought you were my McDonald's delivery."

Harvey's eyes flick down and clock the fact I'm in my boxers.

"I was about to take a shower," I explain. "I was up late."

Harvey nods. "Jas said to meet her here?"

"She did?"

"We're gonna walk over to archery together," he says.

"You do archery?" I say. "With Jas? She never said."

Harvey squints at me. "Why would she? There's, like, thirty of us."

"Just seems weird she wouldn't say."

He blows out a breath. "It's ... really no big deal. Is Jas here or not?"

I nod.

There's a sort of stand-off between me and Harvey at the door.

"Can I come in then?" he asks eventually.

I nod again, and he squeezes past me. "Sonic fan, are you?" Harvey asks.

"Huh?"

He gestures to my boxers, which display a large illustration of said hedgehog.

"Emergency pair," I tell Harvey. "I ran out of clean underwear." I cringe at myself, babbling on about dirty laundry. "Jas is in the lounge – go in."

Harvey smirks and saunters off, but I swear he cops an extra glance at Sonic before he does. Great, I love giving the impression that I've got the mentality of a twelve year old.

I take a deep breath and beat myself up about how I'm here in my underwear, with bed-head hair. I haven't even brushed my teeth yet. Then I follow Harvey in. He's standing by the window, stretching an arm behind his back. "Sorry, came from the gym," Harvey explains to Jas. His T-shirt has ridden up, revealing his abs and the waistband of his boxers – Calvin Klein, of course, because he's not a total embarrassment to himself. "Ready to shoot some arrows?" he continues.

"Mm, like *Cupid*," Jas replies, really pointedly.

I glare at her, partly because she needs to shut up and partly because she's kept Harvey's presence at archery a secret from me. If I'd known, I might have joined.

"Cupid?" Harvey says. "Aw, hardly. Not much love happening anywhere near me right now." He stuffs his hands in his pockets and looks down at the floor.

I nod meaningfully. "I just wanted to say, I heard the sad news about you and Summer. I'm very, very sorry."

"Thanks, mate," Harvey says, looking up again. "I guess we just drifted apart, or whatever."

His eyes meet mine and I feel this fizzing in my stomach, so I panic and quickly flop down on the sofa. I place a cushion over my lap before it's obvious how much I really like him. "Well, anyway, if there's anything I can do ..." I say, but trail off because what can I actually do?

I'm a mess and everyone knows it. I can't help Harvey Ledger. What a joke.

I'm a joke.

Everyone else is getting on with their lives.

Jas has a date to prom.

Harvey goes to the gym.

I think both of them have brushed their teeth this morning.

And suddenly this feels like a watershed moment. Like one of those pivotal moments in your life, a fork in the road. You can choose which way to go, but one way leads to success and happiness, and the other leads to ... well, eating Big Macs in your boxers while watching porn on your laptop.

That second road might be fun, and totally what I had planned for the next half hour, but maybe I don't want it to be my entire life, you know?

It's suddenly crystal clear. I need to take positive action. And sure, what I'm about to ask Harvey is massive. And it's scary. But if I don't ...

Plus, I'm at rock bottom. Right now, I couldn't look any worse if I tried. So I have nothing to lose. I'm going to prom alone anyway, so why not shoot for the stars like Jas and Mrs Harper and everyone else says?

And maybe no one else *has* asked Harvey yet. What do they say? *Right place, right time?*

So I dress it up like it's a joke. I smile, and I kind of laugh, all casual, not serious, and I say, "Like, if you need a prom date ...?"

Harvey is staring at me.

I swallow.

There's this terrible silence. So I add, in a small voice, "I'll ... be your prom date?"

The weird silence fills the room, my words just hanging in the air.

Jas isn't breathing. I'm not breathing.

I'm not sure if Harvey is breathing; he's just ... staring at me.

I can't read the expression on his face.

I swallow.

Is Harvey going to hit me?

I think he's going to hit me!

And then Harvey seems to shake himself back to reality, takes a breath and raises his eyebrows. He says ...

CHAPTER 3

"OK then."

CHAPTER 4

"What?" I say weakly.

Harvey gives a little shrug, which isn't the clear response I need at this point.

"Huh?" I say. I don't understand. Harvey didn't just agree to go to prom with me. He couldn't have done. Why would he? He's the hottest boy in school. He could ask anyone, even someone who already has a date, and they would drop their plans and choose him.

Harvey gives me a small smile. I wouldn't call it wide, or even particularly happy. His smile is more ... cautious? Possibly ... *sly?*

And then it hits me. It's a joke. It has to be.

Harvey's agreed to be my date, but he doesn't mean it, because it was such a ridiculous question. So ridiculous, he gave a ridiculous answer.

Top-tier banter.

So I laugh.

I laugh for a good ten seconds.

And then I stop and realise he's just staring at me.

"Sorry, I thought you were serious," Harvey says.

"He was serious," Jas pipes up.

"Were you serious?" Harvey demands.

My mouth is dry. Too dry to form words, so I nod.

Harvey squints at me and says, "It's prom. You don't dick about with prom. If you didn't mean it—"

"I'm not ... dicking about," I assure him.

"You want to go to prom with me?" Harvey asks.

"I want to go to prom with you," I manage to squeak. *What is happening?*

"Right," he says.

I don't know if I should laugh or cry. I don't understand.

Jas has this smug look on her face, like she's responsible for the matchmaking feat of the decade. I'm not sure I share her confidence about this. I feel like I need Harvey to write all this down. A contract. Signed and sealed. To confirm he has actually agreed to take me to prom as his date.

I'll say it again.

Harvey Ledger, a straight boy (and I'm sure he is straight), wants to take little gay me (Alfie Parker) to prom as his *date*.

I'm not a fool. Life isn't a fairy tale. Not for people like me anyway. I'm not expecting a happy ending here – it will all go wrong. The whole thing will be shown to be a complex hoax, forever remembered on everyone's phones and uploaded to TikTok. But when that happens, I want it *in writing* that this was meant to be real and I had no reason to think otherwise.

Harvey sniffs and looks at me. "When shall we meet then?"

I shrug. "I dunno," I reply. "Like half an hour before prom starts?"

"Alfie!" Harvey looks super unimpressed. "It's *prom*."

"Yeah?"

"So ... I guess we should plan?" Harvey says. "We're going together, so what were you planning on wearing? We don't want to end up with clashing shirts or something."

"Oh! Right. So, the suit I wore to my granddad's funeral. It should still fit."

He stares at me. "You're going to wear *death clothes*?"

"I've tried to tell him," Jas says, shaking her head. That's a lie, because she hasn't, but I'll take it up with her later when golden boy isn't here. I have to be on my best behaviour right now.

"And what do you mean, 'It should still fit'? You haven't tried it on yet?" Harvey continues.

"I mean, it might be a little short in the leg," I say. "I've grown since Year Nine, but—"

"Lemme stop you there," Harvey says. "A special night deserves special effort. Maybe we get matching handkerchiefs, you know? What about waistcoats? The theme's *Alice in Wonderland*, so is there anything we could add to our outfits that's a nod towards that?"

I stare at him blankly.

"Exactly," Harvey says. "Which is why we should plan. Trust me, some people are going all-out on this. You wanna make a splash, don't you?"

I nod.

"Good. You free tomorrow?" Harvey asks.

"... Yes?"

"Good. Meet me at Starbucks at eleven and we'll go shopping. Sort some bits out." Harvey pulls his phone out, checks the time and looks at Jas. "We'll be late."

Jas grabs her bag and stands up. "See you later, Alf. You should come to archery sometime ... but knowing you, you'd only try to *shoot yourself in the foot!*" Jas cocks her head towards Harvey and uses her fingers to pull her

mouth into a smile. I think she's suggesting that I need to be happier about all this.

"Sure," I say. "Oh, and Harvey?"

He turns at the door to look at me, his eyebrows raised.

"Um ... I'm really excited? About this?" I continue. "Over-excited, actually!"

His eyes flick to the cushion on my lap and he smirks. "Are you now?"

And just like that, Harvey Ledger strolls out of my house. What's more, he's whistling a perky little tune to himself like none of the last five minutes is the most monumental, earth-shattering stuff ever.

I hear the front door slam shut and sit in silence for a minute, trying to take it all in.

I didn't just bag the hottest boy in the school as my prom date.

I couldn't have.

Could I?

CHAPTER 5

THREE DAYS TO PROM

I'm trying to act totally chill about the fact I'm sitting opposite Harvey Ledger in Starbucks. Spoiler: I am *not* chill. I am a bag of nerves and excitement. This is not helped by the fact I didn't get much sleep again last night. There was too much bouncing around my head.

I replayed the conversation with Harvey in different ways, trying to work out if I'd missed something, or interpreted his answer incorrectly. I came to a conclusion: maybe it's true. Maybe you *do* have to shoot for the stars. Maybe, if you try, sometimes you succeed. I'm not saying it would work every time, and maybe this was just beginner's luck, but maybe Harvey really *does* want to go to prom with me.

Wilder things do happen to people.

Folk win the lottery all the time, even when the odds are stacked against them.

Maybe, this time, I've won.

I've bloody won!

Starbucks is busy, but a woman with kids lets me and Harvey go ahead of her in the queue, saying, "We'll be ages choosing a cake." The barista squeezes extra caramel sauce on our Frappuccinos, then a table becomes free at the exact second we've paid and walk into the seating area. I'm not imagining it: the universe is smiling on us, on me. I dunno, maybe it's smiling mainly on Harvey and a bit of the sparkle is hitting me too. It doesn't matter; the point is, this feels *good*.

"Now, we need to keep this a secret, cause we don't want anyone stealing our idea," Harvey says, slurping his drink. "What are your thoughts on pocket watches? You know, those ones on gold chains that hang from waistcoats?"

"It's not something I often think about," I reply.

Harvey laughs, then frowns. "You get why I'm asking?"

I must look panicked because he chuckles and playfully reaches over and ruffles my hair. It's an action that both turns me to jelly and gives me a hard-on. "Oh, Alfie," Harvey says. "The prom theme! *Alice in Wonderland*. The Mad Hatter has one."

"Has what?"

"A pocket watch!" he almost howls.

"Ohhhh," I say.

"Real ones would be expensive, but I wonder if we could get a couple from a fancy-dress shop?"

Harvey starts checking Google for nearby fancy-dress shops and a message flashes up on my phone:

JAS: *Summer is on the warpath. Just to warn you.*

So, *great*. You might be thinking, *Well, so what?* But Summer is a girl who once managed to get a teacher fired for grading one of her essays below average. And Summer's family once sued a well-known fast-food chain for serving coffee that was too hot and burned her mum's mouth a bit ...

I wanted to ask, *Why didn't she drink it more carefully? It's coffee – of course it's hot!* What I'm saying is, the best legal team in the world can't help against Summer Gray and her family – so I stand no chance.

Harvey must spot the look of despair on my face because he cocks his head at me. "What's up?"

"Nothing," I reply.

"Show me," he says, glancing at my phone.

I show him the message, and he rolls his eyes. "Don't worry about Summer. It's me she's angry with. Nothing to do with you."

"Sure," I say, but I don't believe him.

"Honestly, let me handle Summer," Harvey says.

"Sure," I say again. Again, I don't believe him. Or rather, I don't believe he can handle her, but, whatever – it's happening now. I'll just have to man up and accept my fate.

"Let's shop!" Harvey declares, getting up. "We can drink these as we go – keep our energy up!"

I've no idea why he isn't more worried. Maybe he's never really appreciated what Summer is capable of. Anyway, maybe Harvey needs to find that out for himself, so I grab my drink and we head out into the street.

I've always been a fashion disaster, so I'm grateful that Harvey is leading this thing. We spend about an hour zipping in and out of various shops on the high street "for inspiration" and end up in the menswear section of Graham's department store.

Harvey looks through rails of clothes, holding up various waistcoats for me to comment on and putting pairs of smart black trousers against me.

I just nod and make appreciative noises, because how should I know what looks good?

I know, I know, I'm gay, so the general belief is I should know about this sort of stuff. But I don't. And Harvey does. And he's straight. (Or meant to be.) So, go figure.

"What do you think of this shirt?" Harvey asks, holding up a pale blue one.

"Suits you," I reply. *(But also, a sack would suit you, because you're perfect, you doofus!)*

"Yeah?" He smiles. "I'm gonna quickly try it on. Wait here. Don't get into any trouble!" Harvey winks at me and disappears towards the fitting rooms, while I grin at the fact he winked like that. I'm getting way ahead of myself, but I'm really enjoying this. I'm loving his company and, yeah, I know I shouldn't, but I'm kind of imagining us as boyfriends and it feels really nice.

It's OK to dream, right?

I turn and start flicking through another rail of clothes, not really sure what I'm looking for, but humming contentedly. I'm fully imagining me and Harvey living together in New York, or something. You know, strolling around Central Park with flat whites, designer clothes and a small dog.

I sweep five shirts to the left and it's suddenly like a horror movie. There's Summer Gray's face, staring at me from the other side of the rail.

I stifle a squeal.

And then she's next to me. "Hello, *Alfie*," Summer says.

My whole body tenses. Really, it's worse than that – I nearly piss myself, but let's gloss over *that*, because it's gross.

31

"Summer!" I say. "Hi! What are you doing here?"

"I'm shopping, Alfie," Summer replies. "Shopping for prom. I *should* be shopping with my date, the love of my life, my boyfriend since *birth*, Harvey Ledger. Do you know him? Oh! Of course you do, because, like some vulture, you couldn't wait to get your teeth into the dying remains of our relationship!"

I'm frozen, staring at her.

"How dare you?" Summer continues. "You've preyed on Harvey at his most vulnerable! He was reeling from our temporary break-up, doubtless feeling lonely and afraid. Then you come along and ask him out at his very weakest, *in his darkest hour*!"

"I just thought he might need a new date for prom," I bleat.

"Well, he doesn't!" Summer says. "Because he has me!"

"I thought you dumped him?"

She screws her face up like I'm chatting nonsense. "*Yes*, Alfie, I did dump him. To remind Harvey that he shouldn't take me for granted.

And if he'd had time to reflect, he would have seen his mistake and realised his love for me. He would have made the sort of prom-posal I think any girl in my position deserves!"

"But—"

"Jesus!" Summer cuts me off. "Just stop interfering in other people's lives, Alfie!"

"But—"

She leans into me. "He isn't gay, you know? If you're thinking he's going to so much as kiss you, nah-ah! Won't happen. He's just really nice. That's why some people *think* he's gay. But he isn't. Trust me – *I know*."

I glance over my shoulder. *How long does it take to try a shirt on?*

"But also," Summer continues, her voice dripping with poison, "I don't want you to get hurt. You know he's using you, right?"

I frown. "Using me? How?"

"Oh, Alfie, Alfie." Summer shakes her head sadly, like I'm so naive. "Harvey is a straight teenage boy! It's all about the 'banter' ... *innit?* It's all a joke to him and his mates. The next big laugh. To totally own one of the LGBTQ+ kids they dislike so much but can't ever admit to hating because they're not allowed to be homophobic these days."

Summer looks at me like I'm total shit. "It's a bit of fun at your expense, Alfie," she says. "Because why else would Harvey be doing this?"

CHAPTER 6

"OK," Harvey says, putting down his shopping bags in the middle of TK Maxx half an hour later. "Are you going to tell me what's going on?"

Summer vanished as fast as she'd appeared. Two minutes after she'd gone, Harvey emerged from the fitting room, having decided the shirt wasn't right after all.

I'd decided not to mention seeing Summer – it had been a nice day so far and I didn't want anything to bring us down. In my heart, I knew she was just being bitter and trying to stir up trouble. But in my head, all I could think was that Summer was telling the truth, and this explained *everything*.

Hadn't I been puzzled as to why Harvey would agree to be my prom date at first? I'd tried to pretend it was just a case of shooting for the stars and hitting the bullseye, but didn't Summer's explanation make more sense?

Lads love banter.

I'd tried to push those thoughts out of my head as we paid for our stuff and strolled around a few more shops. But the paranoia started to grow; the doubts multiplied. I became convinced I was nothing but the fall guy in Harvey's comedic long con.

"... Because you've been really weird since we left the department store," Harvey continues, crossing his arms like he means business.

Huh. He sure is perceptive for a straight boy.

He cocks his head and adds, "So?"

The middle of TK Maxx wouldn't be my ideal location for a heart-to-heart, but we're here now and it's happening, so I suppose I have to just go with it. But I can't just accuse Harvey of using me. Or even hint at it. He'd just deny it anyway and, besides, it would hardly mark me out as a trusting, low-maintenance prom date.

Like, it's only been twenty-four hours since he agreed to go to prom with me and I'm already accusing him of some scheme to make his mates laugh? I wouldn't date me.

"I just wondered," I begin, "why you agreed to go with me? To prom?"

Harvey narrows his eyes slightly. He's suspicious, I think. "Cause you asked," he replies.

"That's it?"

"That's it," Harvey says. "But it's a pretty big 'it', Alfie."

"I know it is. I was the one asking!"

Harvey laughs at that. "No, I know," he says. "It's just ... I knew Summer wanted me to ask her to prom, and to make a huge deal out of asking her. She's been dropping hints since the end of Year Ten. But why couldn't Summer ask me?"

"I guess that's the way it's always been done," I say. "The boy asks the girl."

He snorts. "Oh, right. So, what if two girls or two boys go to prom – who's meant to ask then? And even if it's a boy and girl, why shouldn't the girl ask?"

I nod because I know he's right.

Harvey sighs. "Summer's got all these fixed ideas about how things are 'meant' to be. It always feels like they're designed to make her feel special – give her those Instagram-worthy moments she's so desperate to share. And I get it – everyone should feel special sometimes. But what about me? Don't I get to feel that too? Feel like I'm worth making a bit of effort for?" Harvey chuckles. "Sorry, this is *way* too deep and a massive downer. Let's just say: you asked, which was nice, cause no one's ever asked me out before; it's always been me doing the asking. So I said yes. You OK with that?"

I smile and nod.

But I still have questions. Questions that feel too big to ask. Such as ...

So, we're just doing this as mates, right?

You don't actually fancy me?

It's a "date" but not in a romantic way?

And if all that's the case ...

How come you're so chill about what people think? Don't you worry that people might call you gay?

Or ...

Is that all fine because it's all part of the joke?

Just like Summer said.

I can't shake the feeling that none of this is real. It doesn't matter how charming Harvey is, how much he seems to be "in" to chatting with me. I don't believe it.

Harvey sighs. "What else?"

"Huh?"

"There's something else."

I shake my head.

"Alfie?" Harvey presses.

"OK, look, back in the department store ... Summer was there. She ... spoke to me. She ..."

Harvey's staring right at me, but I can't make eye contact, so I drop my gaze to the floor. "She told me you're only going to prom with me for banter," I say. "So ..."

I'm still staring at the floor.

When I do finally look back up, Harvey's eyes are full of sadness, and my heart breaks a little.

"Have I ever been a dick to you?" he asks.

"Um, no."

"Because if I have, I'm sorry."

"No, you haven't," I say.

"I wouldn't do something like that," Harvey tells me. "I'm not saying I'm perfect, cause I'm not sure anyone is, but I'm over 'banter'. I respect people. I respect *you*. I'm not some arrogant lad whose idols are wankers with fast cars on TikTok and who thinks it's all about *me*."

I feel terrible. "I'm sorry. I know that. It's just—"

"*Summer*," Harvey says. "I know. She knows how to get a reaction."

I nod. "I'm sorry."

He takes a deep breath. "People talk shit. And me and you going to prom? Well, I guess people are gonna talk a lot of shit about that."

"Yeah," I say. "And how do you feel about that?"

Harvey chews his lip, lost in thought, his brow furrowed. Eventually, he meets my eyes again.

"Not bothered, I guess?" Harvey says, then looks away. "Just gossip, right?"

"Right," I say. But I'm not so sure. I'm used to people chatting shit about me – it kind of goes hand-in-hand with being gay and out at school. But I don't think someone like Harvey has ever experienced what it's like to be on the receiving end of that. The whispers. The little glances. The nasty smiles. I wonder if he's ready for it? Only time will tell. For now, there's just one thing I need to know.

"So we're doing this, for real?" I ask.

Harvey Ledger looks me right in the eyes and he says ...

CHAPTER 7

"For real."

CHAPTER 8

Harvey's answer puts a smile on my face for the rest of our shopping trip. Still, it isn't long before my head starts to come up with more questions, like:

What part of it is real?

We're going to prom, that much is real, so did he mean that?

Or is it more than that?

Could it be real like ... romantic real?

And then I tell myself to STFU! because I know I'm overthinking all of this. Harvey hasn't said he's anything other than straight. Even if he wasn't, not everyone is going to prom with someone they fancy anyway. Before Jas asked Joe Chan, she was going to prom with me, for example, and that wasn't romantic. A few other people's dates are "just friends". A bunch of the rugby lads are all "going together", and I doubt very much they're involved in some sort of polyamorous relationship with one another.

I spend *way* too much time thinking about that.

By the time I'm home, I've promised myself not to overthink any of this. I'm going to prom with Harvey. For real. It's not a joke. It's just a thing we've decided to do.

So let's leave it at that.

And then Summer strikes again.

It's 11 p.m. and she's all over social media. Summer has released a video of herself, all red puffy eyes and tears streaming down her cheeks. Between her sobs and gulps of air, I can just make out what she's saying:

"It's literally ... three days until prom ... and all my life ... just wanted a ... fairy-tale ending ..." Summer bleats. "Every girl ... wants to feel like a princess and ... Harvey Ledger ... ruined everything ... callous ... Now ... *Alfie Parker* ... honest to god, you've never seen such a tragic loser in all your life … couldn't wait to invite Harvey to prom himself … Harvey would normally never agree to that, but he's … clearly upset … not in his right mind … So now Alfie is using Harvey to gain popularity … so obvious … so devious … stolen *my* boyfriend … We've been together since we were in the womb … so now I'm alone. All alone. On prom night." Cue ugly crying.

She's added a track from *Grease* to her reel, so "It's Raining on Prom Night" is accompanying all this – like it wasn't already completely over the top. She's currently getting a great many likes on Instagram and TikTok, as well as comments, which are calling me things like "opportunistic", "a boyfriend snatcher" and "massive bell-end".

I really want to respond. I want to write in the comments: *Hey, I did ask Harvey, but he also said yes! It takes two to tango!* But I don't think there's any point. More concerning are some of the other comments

Joshy2008: *I'll talk some sense into Harvey.*

JakeTheRake: *Leave it to the lads, Summer. We got you!*

Sophfrompluto: *You are such a strong, beautiful woman, Summer. Harvey will come to his senses! (If you still want him, of course, but you could have anyone!) Everyone loves you. Everyone admires you. Alfie Parker is such a simp. And he looks about twelve. Harvey will see that soon and come back begging.*

I throw my phone across my bed and swallow the hard lump in my throat. Look, it's true, I'm not one of those fit gym lads that are everywhere online. If I had to rate myself, I'd be about a six out of ten. And Harvey would be a nine. Oh, who am I kidding? I'd be a three and Harvey would be a ten. The point is, yes, he's all-round more attractive and buff and hotter than I am, but I'm mostly OK with that.

I spent about two years wishing I had a less lanky, better proportioned body, and I've come out the other side. So, I don't really care what people say about me or what they think I'm "worthy" of. Why should Summer be the only one to have a "fairy-tale ending"? Why shouldn't I? I don't think I've done anything wrong. I only asked Harvey to prom.

But their words eat away at me. However hard I try to ignore them.

Harvey will read them too.

And what if he starts to see their point?

Everyone laughing at him being with me?

Because I'm so pathetic-looking?

I don't want that.

I'll feel proud to be at prom with Harvey.

And he'll feel embarrassed.

That can't happen.

I'm going to have to do something.

CHAPTER 9

TWO DAYS TO PROM

It's 9 a.m. and I'm in the gym, attempting to bench-press 10kg. Which is really hard, it turns out.

All right, I know, prom is in two days. I'm not going to be able to radically change myself in that time. I'm not suddenly going to bulk up, tone up and get some muscles. But that's not the point. *I'm trying.* I'm making changes. I'm trying to show Harvey that I can be different – that he doesn't need to be embarrassed around me, because I'm going to be better. Really soon. As soon as I can manage to lift this bar up from my chest.

I kind of hate that I'm doing this for *him* and not for *me*, but then fitness is a good thing, right?

It's a healthy thing. So, actually, maybe I am doing this for me, and Harvey has just spurred me on.

Or maybe this is what it's like when you start caring about something.

Or ... *someone*.

Oh god. I push *that* thought away pretty fast and remind myself we're *friends*. Harvey and I are going to prom as *friends*.

This bar doesn't want to budge. And there are no actual weights on it – it's the bar alone that weighs 10kg. Even that is too much for me.

I try to tell myself I can do it. Gear myself up mentally. Imagine myself as a muscly Greek god. That's meant to help, right?

It does not help.

And then I hear his voice.

Harvey.

He's chatting to one of his mates. I can't tell which one, but Harvey is here, in the gym. Of course he is. Of course Harvey works out every morning, because he's a successful, healthy, popular, happy person who should probably be with someone who is also successful, healthy, popular and happy ...

No! I tell myself. *You cannot think like that!*

I don't want Harvey to see me. Not like this – all weak and pathetic. I don't want him to think I'm a crap excuse of a human. Other people are attracted to successful people, right? That's how it works. Like moths to light – you've gotta *shine.* Or at least make others think you do. I'll just drop into conversation later with Harvey that I'm working out – keep it casual, like it's no big deal. But it'll plant the seed. And, crucially, he won't have to see the reality of it.

I slide out from under the bar of the bench press, scoot over and sit on the floor with my back to the wall. I put my towel over my head, like I'm *bushed* and just resting for a bit.

"Mate, we need to talk about this *Alfie* thing."

I recognise the voice of Harvey's mate now. It's Joe Chan. Jas's date to prom.

Why am I a "thing"?

"What about Alfie?" Harvey says.

"Bro, everyone's gonna think you're gay for a start," says Joe.

"So what?" Harvey asks.

Joe laughs. "All right, well, that's on you. But why go to prom with Alfie when Summer's right there?"

Harvey doesn't respond to that, unless I can't hear what he says. But it's clear to me that Joe is a total *dick* when he thinks no one else is listening.

I know why Jas asked Joe to prom. At school, around everyone else, Joe plays the sensitive, charming card. In reality, I'm sensing he's one of those "no homo" straight lads. You know the kind – who think their masculinity is under threat if they get told misogyny is bad or there's so much as an LGBTQ+ book in the school library.

"You've been with Summer since you were little kids," Joe continues.

"I mean, that's not true, that was just our parents," Harvey says. "Anyway, *Summer* dumped me."

"Yeah, to test your reaction! Don't you get that? She felt, I dunno ... like you'd lost interest, maybe. So, Summer wanted to see how you'd react. Sometimes people need to know how you feel about them. It's all a game, man. And you just lost. Big time."

"Yeah, well," Harvey says. "Wanna go first? I'll count reps."

"No," Joe says. "I wanna get this sorted. What's with Alfie?"

"Nothing."

"Do you like him?"

I hear Harvey chuckle, but I can tell it's a nervous chuckle. "Mate, he's all right, OK?" Harvey says.

"That's not what I meant."

Harvey sighs and I can picture him crossing his arms.

"I'm gonna ask you something," Joe continues. "Something big. And we've been mates since forever, so you know you can trust me. You know you can be honest, yeah?"

There's a pause.

"Are you gay for Alfie Parker?" Joe says.

My breath catches as I wait for Harvey's reply. This is it, the thing I really want to know, and, great news, it's not even me having to ask this one, it's Joe. It kind of feels like a win, despite now being in possession of knowledge that reveals Joe Chan to be a prick – something I'm going to *have* to share with Jas at some point, which feels like a lose.

But there's this weird silence and I'm straining to hear. I'm starting to think that maybe they've walked away to another piece of equipment, but then I hear …

"Alfie? Is that you?"

I don't know why, but I keep the towel over my head, like maybe Harvey will lose confidence and assume he's got it wrong if I don't respond.

But he doesn't give up.

"I kind of feel those are definitely your socks," Harvey says.

Damn it. I don't know what's worse: the fact I own (and am wearing) Sonic the Hedgehog socks, or the fact Harvey thinks that I'm the only person of our age who would wear such things.

I pull the towel off. "Oh! Hi!" I say. "Yes, these are my socks. My normal ones are in the wash." I nod. "I'm just working out. How are you?"

"Never seen you in here before," Harvey says.

"Just joined."

He raises his eyebrows and says, "Yeah?"

I mean, I think that means he's pleased. I *knew* it! I knew this was the right thing to do. And maybe it's good that Harvey spotted me because now I don't even need to mention it casually and risk it sounding anything but.

"I'm bulking up a bit!" I laugh. "Toning those ..." I can't remember the name, so I point to my stomach.

"Abs?" Harvey suggests.

I click my fingers. "Bingo! Abs! Abductors!"

"Abdominals," Harvey corrects me.

"Yep, those too. *Abs*-olutely! All the abs!" I grin at him, then glance at Joe, who has his hands on his hips, frowning at us.

"I didn't think you cared about that sort of stuff?" Harvey says.

I don't know what to say to that, because he's right, I don't, but I'm not sure how Harvey knows that. Is it because I'm so clearly unfit and weak-looking? Frankly, that's all the more reason to do this then!

"Just thought I'd tone up for the summer," I say breezily. And then I add, just as breezily, "I'd look better, don't you think?"

My eyes meet Harvey's. He gives me this small, sweet smile, shrugs and says ...

CHAPTER 10

"I think you look good as you are, but if it makes you happy, go for it."

CHAPTER 11

I mean, Harvey's reply is *hilarious*. He's obviously just being nice, but it's sweet of him anyway.

I know my cheeks have gone bright red.

Joe Chan scowls at Harvey and says, "Oh my god, why are you trying to rizz him up?"

Harvey replies, "I'm not trying to rizz him up!"

I really need to get out of here. I make my excuses and say I'm just going to "cool down for three minutes on the treadmill" and then head home. There's no point in being miserable in the gym if Harvey isn't even bothered by my abs, or lack thereof.

I give Harvey a little wave as I head out. He calls over, "You at home this afternoon?"

"Uh-huh," I reply.

"I'll come over about two. I found some pocket watches in a charity shop!" Harvey lowers his voice a bit, I guess since this was meant to be a secret and here he is announcing it in the gym. "Nice ones too," Harvey goes on. "We're gonna look great, but I want to see how we attach them before the big day!"

I nod, but, honestly, I would have nodded whatever he'd said. He could have said, "We should go and dig up radioactive waste for a laugh, don't you think?" and I legit think I would have agreed to the plan.

I smile and say, "See you later then!"

"See you, Alfie."

And then I make the mistake of glancing at Joe. There's a split second before he notices me looking and puts the "nice" mask on, and, honestly, he looks so furious, and so pissed off, you'd think Joe wanted to take Harvey as his date to prom himself. Normally, that would worry me, but somehow, Harvey has made me feel bulletproof.

When I get home, I shower, wash and condition and style my hair. Then I pluck my eyebrows and generally spruce myself up ready for Harvey's visit. I may be "fine as I am", but surely there are limits?

I get some snacks ready (Pringles – decanted from tube and arranged on plate) and light a scented candle (lavender). Then I make a Spotify playlist that hopefully speaks to my interesting and eclectic choice in music. (It includes Elvis, Queen, R.E.M., Oasis, Beyoncé, Lady Gaga, Steps, the entire soundtrack of *Wicked*, and "Come On Eileen" by … well, whoever sang it. I just know the song from way too many family weddings over the years.)

Then, because I like to ruin nice moments when I'm almost feeling OK about myself, I make the mistake of quickly checking social media.

Summer has posted her big prom-posal to none other than Peter Popper and it's gone viral. Peter is a chess geek with little interest in personal hygiene. He currently has his arm in a sling after falling down half a flight of stairs when he slipped on a pawn that fell out of the chess set he was carrying.

What I'm saying is: I'm a dork. But Peter is worse.

Nevertheless, someone has filmed Summer approaching Peter outside the Warhammer shop on the high street and asking him to prom. Peter looks shell-shocked, mutters "OK?" and then Summer tells Peter he may kiss her. He gives her a very nervous peck on the cheek. In return, she launches into a full-blown snog.

Thirty seconds later, Peter comes up for air, red-faced, sweaty and unable to speak or stand up properly. The video cuts to a montage sequence featuring Summer pulling Peter around various shops and the barber's. Then the words "Glow up complete!" appear on screen and Brand-New Peter is introduced.

I'll be damned if he doesn't look quite hot. He's got a quiff thing going on and a new suit that gives him a James Bond vibe. Even the sling is somehow now sexy and gives Peter a rugged quality, like he legit might have been injured fighting assassins in the SAS.

There's a close-up of Summer at the very end, smiling down the lens of the camera. "Too bad,

Harvey Ledger," she says. "You just got Peter Poppered!"

It's manipulative, it's tacky and it's so obvious what this is. Project: Make Harvey Jealous.

I just hope Harvey doesn't fall for it. Still, I spend the next few hours fretting about him doing exactly that – running round to Summer's house, getting down on his knees, begging her to take him back and so on.

But Harvey turns up at mine just after two, like he said he would, with his rucksack and a suit carrier.

"Daffodils!" Harvey says, sniffing the air.

"*Lavender*," I correct him.

"I knew it smelled familiar. My mum puts that in her essential oil burner when she's stressed." Harvey's eyes meet mine. "Are you stressed?"

"Not at all!" I chirp.

"You liar. You thought I might fall for Summer's attempt at making me jealous." Harvey grins at me and boops me on the nose. "You're so transparent, Alfie."

I giggle because *he booped me on the freakin' nose.* I manage to compose myself and say, "I mean ... I did see it online."

"It's like she's gaslighting me!" Harvey says as we walk into my lounge. "*Summer* dumped *me*," he continues. "So, saying I've been 'Peter Poppered' isn't the massive own she thinks it is – it's not like she gave me a choice." Harvey flops down on the sofa.

"If she hadn't dumped you, you'd still be going to prom with her?" I say, sitting down opposite him.

He shrugs. "I guess."

"And ... you'd want to?" I ask.

"I dunno," he says glumly. "It's always just been expected. Mum and Dad always called Summer my 'girlfriend' since before I could even talk. That's even how they introduced us to other people at parties and barbecues and stuff: 'This is our son, Harvey, and his little girlfriend, Summer!' Everyone would think it was so sweet and go 'Aw!' and 'Ahh!' But actually ... it really pissed me off. She seemed to like it though." Harvey meets my eyes. "Interesting, the things we get told we have to be, isn't it?"

And, *wow*, isn't it? The truth of that hits me hard. Like gender-reveal parties, which I always think are a tad presumptuous. Or the kids who get told they have to go to church – to think *this*, or do *that*. So much of it is about creating some mini-me version of your parents. But we're not our parents. We're us. We're different. And we should get to make our own choices.

But it's not just our parents. Sometimes it's *us* too. We do it to each other. "Joe Chan thinks you and Summer belong together too," I mutter.

"Ohhh," he replies. "So, you did hear that. I was worried you might have."

"In the gym, yeah," I reply. "I couldn't help it."

"Yeah, well. Everyone's got opinions, haven't they? Joe will get over it. Hopefully my parents will too."

I raise my eyebrows because *that* sounds like a whole new level of crap that Harvey's dealing with.

"Well," he says, "you can imagine they aren't happy, right? They've been planning mine and Summer's wedding since the day we were born.

I'm not kidding. Summer's parents have a deposit down on Kingsley Hall for the reception."

"Shit! Really?" I say.

Harvey nods. "Anyway, I think Summer and Peter make a lovely couple. They're welcome to Kingsley Hall, so the money won't be wasted. I will be cheering them on at prom. And hey, maybe one day my parents will decide they don't hate me after all."

He takes an unsteady breath, then sighs.

"Are you OK?" I ask.

"Not really," Harvey replies. "Apparently, I've brought 'shame' on the family. I'm not exactly sure why. But we're doing this now, so screw 'em all, right?"

"I mean, if—" I start to say.

"No ifs, no buts," Harvey says quickly. His eyes soften. "Have you got your waistcoat and suit jacket?"

"Upstairs."

"Wanna try out these?" Harvey fishes two gold pocket watches out of his rucksack – nice ones, actually. They even tell the real time.

I'm glad we're not talking about everyone else any more and this is about us. We head up the stairs and into my bedroom. I'm suddenly super conscious that Harvey is in my space now, *the bedroom*, and we all know what can happen in bedrooms.

I try not to think about that and get the waistcoat and jacket out from my wardrobe and put them on over my T-shirt. He's brought his waistcoat and jacket in the suit carrier, so he puts his on too. Then we turn to face each other, and Harvey places the watch in the pocket of my waistcoat and fumbles around trying to thread the chain through the middle buttonhole.

It takes him a few moments, adjusting the gold chain, moving it about. I watch him – so focused, so gentle, *so close to me.* The closest we've even been. My breathing is unsteady. There's a buzzing in my ears. I don't want this to end.

Harvey hands me the other watch.

"Go on then," he says.

So, I do the same, placing it into the pocket of his waistcoat, adjusting the chain just like he did. My hands are shaking. I hope he doesn't notice.

"There," I mutter.

We both turn to face the mirror and I almost gasp. We look *so* good. Handsome. Despite both being in jeans and T-shirts with the waistcoats and jackets on top – it's not even the full suit or anything. And I realise it's not about the clothes. We look ... *happy*. We look young and hopeful and like we've got the world at our feet, and we look ...

We look ...

Like we belong together.

Harvey smiles. He sees it too.

And I smile.

And neither of us know what to do next. It's like the moment is too perfect, and nothing can top it. Except perhaps ...

I become aware of his hand brushing mine.

It's a very gentle question.

It's: *Do you want to hold hands?*

It's: *Do you feel this too?*

It's: *I think I like you. Do you like me?*

My heart leaps into my throat as Harvey's hand brushes mine again. I know now the first time wasn't an accident.

He's asking.

Asking again.

Isn't he?

So I ...

CHAPTER 12

"Ugh! What now?" Harvey mutters.

His phone is ringing.

"Who would be *calling* me, like it's 1994 or something?!" Harvey says.

The moment's broken. I step away, handing him back the pocket watch, the tension releasing as he pulls his mobile out of his jeans pocket.

Harvey's questions about me and him remain unanswered.

But maybe I can answer them in a minute?

I can hear a female voice on the other end, talking rapidly.

"What?" Harvey says quietly down the phone. "When?" His tone is serious. His face is serious.

The whole atmosphere in the room changes. I can't quite place it, but it feels a lot like *fear*.

"Oh god," Harvey mutters. "Yeah, of course, of course." He swallows and returns the phone to his pocket, staring into the middle distance like he's someplace else.

I want to know.

But also … I do *not* want to know. Because something inside me tells me whatever this is might change everything.

There's a charged silence in the air.

I can't stand it any longer.

"Is everything OK?" I ask.

Harvey's eyes meet mine, and they are full of worry and sadness. And he says …

CHAPTER 13

"Summer walked out in front of a bus. She's in hospital. I've gotta get over there."

CHAPTER 14

Harvey bolts out of the house. I try asking him if he needs anything, should I come with him, does he want me to bring anything to the hospital, but he doesn't really answer. He's in a numb panic, and that's understandable.

Harvey was with Summer for the best part of three years.

And now ...

Well, it's unclear what's happened. Harvey wasn't making much sense and I'm not sure anyone really knows the full story anyway. *Summer walked out in front of a bus. An accident? Or ...?*

I swallow the hard lump in my throat. If it was anything other than an accident, and if Summer's reason for doing that was because of

Harvey and prom, then this ends right now. It's not worth it. I really like Harvey, and I really want to go to prom with him, but not if this is what happens.

My head's a mess, so I call Jas – the voice of reason.

"Which hospital?" Jas asks, when I've explained the situation.

"The Kensington," I say.

"*The Kensington?*" she replies. "OK, so that's a private hospital and it doesn't have an A&E department. That makes the story weird because she wouldn't have been rushed there in an ambulance."

"Oh."

"Oh, indeed," Jas says. "Right, well why don't you meet me there? Outside the main entrance."

"Should I bring grapes?" I ask.

"Shut up, Alfie. *Grapes.*" I can totally imagine Jas rolling her eyes. "I don't mean to be cynical, but this is Summer Gray we're talking about. She's done the tears, she's tried to make Harvey jealous, and I guarantee this is just another attempt at manipulation. If she's in the Kensington, that girl has not had a life-threatening accident."

*

A small crowd of Summer's friends has already assembled outside the entrance to the hospital when I arrive. Maybe I imagine it, but it seems like they all look up as one and glare at me, like somehow all this is my fault, like I pushed her in front of the bus myself.

I feel pretty unwelcome, so I keep my distance and sit down on a bench at the far end of the manicured lawns in front of the hospital. It's a very grand building at the end of a long tree-lined driveway. It even has a uniformed porter standing out the front, like a five-star hotel.

I didn't even know this place was here.

Even being sick looks like fun if you're rich.

There's no sign of Jas, so I keep myself busy scrolling social media, and then it pops up. A post from Summer.

It's a photo of her lying in a hospital bed, in one of those patterned surgical gowns. The photo is in black and white for some reason – I guess the seriousness of the situation means colour wouldn't be right.

There's no comment from Summer, but there are a lot from friends and well-wishers: *Sending so much love*; *Thoughts and prayers*; and, of course, the obligatory, *U OK, hun?*

Jas emerges from the hospital entrance and walks directly over to me.

"Good news," I tell her. "Summer has just posted a picture, so I think she's alive."

"Of course she's alive, you utter fool," Jas replies. "I've just dragged the truth out of Joe Chan."

"And?" I say.

"Oh, she walked out in front of a bus all right."

"Oh my god. How awful. On purpose?"

"The bus was stationary," Jas says. "It had stopped at a red light at a *pedestrian crossing*. So, technically, Summer *did* walk out in front of it."

"Right? So, how …?"

"Summer was looking at her phone and tripped on the kerb," Jas tells me.

"So she broke her ankle?" I ask.

Jas sighs. "Nope. Not even sprained it. It just 'hurts a bit'."

I squint at her. "But the ambulance?" I say.

"There was no ambulance, Alfie. Her dad brought her here in his car to be checked over because they have private medical insurance. Places like this will admit anyone for anything if they're willing to pay! He's insisted on an X-ray for his little princess, so that's what they're doing. Don't get me started on the ethics of *that*. The point is, Summer's fine. She's totally fine."

Jas sits down next to me. "She's just played you all. *Again*."

I sit back. Part of me is relieved that I can in no way be blamed for this. But part of me is also angry. Harvey was genuinely worried. Making out you're seriously ill when you're not is really unfair and manipulative. There's probably a technical term for it, but it's basically a real dick move.

Thinking of this reminds me of something. "Jas? I know you asked him to prom and everything, but do you think Joe Chan is a nice guy?" I ask.

She arches an eyebrow at me. "What do you know?" she mutters darkly.

"He was just chatting shit about me in the gym when he thought I wasn't there."

Jas nods solemnly.

"I'm not saying don't go to prom with him," I add. "I'm just saying … be careful? I guess?"

Jas gazes across towards the entrance. An anxious-looking Peter Popper is hovering by himself, clearly not invited to the bedside of his princess.

"Maybe we should all be taking Peter Popper to prom," Jas says wistfully. "He seems like a sweet guy. Maybe we were all wrong about him?"

I'm reminded of what Harvey said earlier about people having roles forced on them. I wonder if we've all been playing parts and those parts are the wrong parts? Some of us playing leads, when really we should be chorus. And some of us in the chorus, who fully deserve being centre stage, are always overlooked. And why? Because what you look like, who your parents are, money and background all add up to what people *expect* of you – and hardly anyone has the bravery to question it.

A little "Ahhh" comes from the crowd of Summer's mates near the entrance as they look at their phones. I guess she's posted something new.

It's a picture of Summer and Harvey. He's sitting by the side of her bed, *holding her hand*. She appears to be connected to a drip, although it's unclear why. The photo is still in black and white, but there's a red heart around the pair of them, with the words *"My knight in shining armour!"* above it.

I swipe the picture away. Am I the villain in someone else's romcom? The evil guy who snatches someone else's boyfriend and, really, Summer was the hero all along, the one everyone was rooting for? And it was looking bad for her, until Summer being rushed to hospital reminded Harvey how much she really meant to him ...

He's *holding her hand.* And the love heart? Has Harvey seen that? Did he approve it? Have they already kissed and made up and mended those bridges?

Are they back together?

Peter Popper seems to think so. After staring at his phone for a full two minutes, he scuttles away, head down, back hunched over, all the charm and shine suddenly gone. Back to his old self.

A big part of me wants to run away too, go back home and hide under my duvet. But I also know I need the answer to my new question, and I may as well get it here and now.

Jas squeezes my hand. "It'll be OK," she tells me.

It's sweet of her. But I don't think it will be. I think Summer has just played her ace card and made Harvey come to his senses. But what about everything in my bedroom earlier? Well, I guess it's amazing what wishful thinking can do to a person, huh? It can make you imagine all sorts of stuff.

An hour later, Summer emerges in a wheelchair, pushed by Harvey. There are ripples of applause and cheers from her friends. Summer takes it all in, smiling, her hair perfect, dressed up to the nines. Meanwhile Harvey just looks shattered, like he's been to hell and back.

I stand up and walk closer, Jas next to me, but I make sure I stay on the outskirts of the group.

"I just want to say a few words," Summer says.

On this cue, all her friends get their phones out and start filming.

"First of all, I want to thank every one of you who has come here today to maintain this vigil outside the hospital," Summer says. "It means the world to me that you all care so much."

"This is Grade A bollocks," Jas mutters.

"Uh huh," I agree.

"Events like today's bring into focus what really matters in life," Summer continues. "And as I lay in my hospital bed, I realised what really matters to me." She twists in the wheelchair to face Harvey. "Harvey Ledger, you are the most wonderful human being – selfless, big-hearted, funny, intelligent, kind and beautiful. You have always been there for me. Even today, after our recent *troubles*, you were still there for me. Because I know you care. And that means so much. So. *Harvey* ..."

I hold my breath for whatever she's about to say.

"Traditionally, it's the boy who asks the girl to prom, usually with a flash mob, or one of those drone light shows if they really care, but you know what? To hell with tradition! Life's short, I know that now, and you've got to grab what you want with both hands! Harvey Ledger," Summer says, "*will you be my date to prom?*"

There's a collective gasp from her friends.

Every phone is trained on Harvey, waiting for his response – the romantic finale to this whole thing.

Some of Summer's mates are already crying tears of joy.

I can't read Harvey's face.

He's looking at her ...

And he opens his mouth ...

Oh god, here it comes ...

And Harvey says ...

CHAPTER 15

"No."

CHAPTER 16

What happens next will totally go viral, but for none of the reasons I assume Summer hoped.

There are about five seconds of shocked silence. Then Summer rises out of her wheelchair like a phoenix from the ashes and begins ranting and swearing at Harvey. She's flailing her arms about wildly as Harvey edges back, like she's a dangerous dog.

After a sentence which contains about ten f-bombs, the whole thing ends with Summer trying to throw her wheelchair at Harvey. (This doesn't really work – it just topples over and skids along the ground.) Then she slumps down (elegantly) on the path, weeping.

I don't even see Harvey go, but he's suddenly vanished.

I make a sharp exit too.

I think I have my answer, but it wouldn't do to stand here smiling like the winner in all this.

CHAPTER 17

ONE DAY TO PROM

The next morning, I leap out of bed cause I'm so full of joy and hope and anticipation.

I *leap*.

I have never *leaped*. I have only ever *slithered* or *rolled* out of bed. Maybe it was exactly what I needed: being brave, asking the big questions and not being afraid of *life*?

Or maybe I just needed someone it was worth taking those risks for?

I haven't heard anything from Harvey since yesterday. I'm guessing he's lying low for a bit, which is fair enough. Still, it suddenly feels like anything is possible and everything is within my grasp.

I even eat some fruit for breakfast.

Well, a strawberry Pop-Tart.

It's like I'm a Brand-New Me!

Jas knocks at my door at ten.

"*Bonjour!*" I trill, opting for French because it sounds so much jollier.

"You need to read this," Jas replies.

She hands me her phone, open on a news article on a trashy gossip website.

And boom! The world comes crashing down.

Prom Queens Set to Take Smithson High School by Storm
By Courtney Sinclair

High school can be a traumatic experience, especially for students at the bottom of the social pecking order. Nothing brings that into sharper focus than the annual tradition of prom.

Some students will enjoy a night to remember with their dates. But others will be left feeling like outcasts and questioning the choices they've made which have led to such tragic outcomes, like no one kissing them during the slow dance.

Popular student Harvey Ledger (16) turned that situation on its head at Smithson High School by asking gay student Alfie Parker to prom. But has what started as an act of charity become something more?

We spoke to Harvey's former long-term girlfriend, Summer Gray, who told us: "Harvey's always thinking of less fortunate people and putting them first. Like, he's always giving food to tramps, and stuff. That's one of the reasons I loved him so much. When Harvey found out Alfie Parker didn't have a date to prom, he told me he was going to do something nice for someone else and ask him."

Harvey is certainly going the extra mile, even buying matching pocket watches for the pair to wear, according to Summer. It has led his friends to speculate there may be more to this arrangement than just charity.

"Prom marks the end of the old and the start of the new," Summer told us. "And I fully support Harvey in this new chapter of his life. I think Harvey is probably gay for Alfie and this is basically Harvey coming out as LGBTQ+ ... or one of the other letters."

Summer continued, "It was either Jesus or Taylor Swift who said, 'Love looks not with the eyes but with the mind.' *That is definitely true.* Like, no offence, but if we were doing a school production of Frankenstein, *Alfie Parker would play the monster.* But I think it's really nice Harvey and Alfie have found love despite such obstacles as a lack of attractiveness. *Looks like we're gonna have two Prom Queens this year!"* she added. "And that's fine because we're all woke, although I don't personally agree with it. It's a bit ick, right? It was Adam and Eve, not Adam and Steve!"

One thing's for sure: whether they win Prom Queens or not, all eyes are going to be on Harvey and Alfie at prom this year!

CHAPTER 18

I swipe the webpage away and stare down at the carpet.

It's already been shared hundreds of times and it only went live half an hour ago.

Everyone at school will have read it.

Then probably a lot of other people within the next few hours.

I don't even care what it says about me – sure, it stings, but I've heard it all before.

It's what it says about Harvey that worries me.

When Harvey arrives at my door ten minutes later, he looks ashen. I don't need to ask why. It's obvious he's read the article too and it's obvious it's had the impact I most feared.

"I had a phone call on my way over," Harvey says. "Some journalist from *Pink and Proud* magazine – they wanted to do a feature on gay kids going to prom." He shakes his head. "I hung up. How did they even get my number?"

"Harvey," I say. I guide him into the lounge, because he looks like he can barely stand. "I'd put money on that article all being the work of Summer herself."

"Totally," Jas agrees. "Anyone can submit an article for that website, and you can totally get away with writing under a fake name – they're really not fussy."

Harvey slumps down into the sofa, his head in his hands. "I know. I worked all that out, but it doesn't matter, does it? Summer is only saying what everyone is thinking. Even my mum came out and asked me this morning, 'Is there anything you want to tell us, Harvey? Are you thinking you might be gay?' Big questions, huh?" Harvey sighs and glances at me. "It'd be great if I knew the answers."

I stare at him. "Wait, you mean, you're—" I say.

"I don't know, OK?!" he snaps. "I don't know what I am. But what I do know is I can't handle everyone discussing it, and analysing it, and wanting me to give them answers that I don't even have yet. And journalists from national magazines? What am I? Some form of entertainment for everyone? Sorry, when did someone's sexuality become anyone's business but theirs?" Harvey sighs and looks down at the floor. "I can't do it. So, I guess Summer's won. I'm sorry, Alfie."

My mouth is dry. "What do you mean?" I ask.

His eyes meet mine and they're full of so much sadness and pain he doesn't need to say it.

But I want him to.

I need him to.

"What do you mean?" I ask him again.

And he says ...

CHAPTER 19

"I'm sorry, but I'm not going to prom with you. I'm not going to go at all."

CHAPTER 20

PROM DAY – 8 A.M.

My eyes pop open the following morning. I'm bolt upright, awake, because that's when it hits me.

Of course.

I'd re-read that article over and over before I fell asleep. Something was off about it, but I couldn't place what. I guess my brain was working overtime while I was asleep, because now I *know*.

I don't even care that it's early and like any respectable teenager he'll still be in bed. I'm up and out of the house in a flash. Twenty minutes later, I'm standing outside his house, hammering on his front door.

"Alfie?" Joe Chan says, wiping sleep from his eyes as he opens the door. He's in boxers and a T-shirt, and looks totally confused. "What are you doing here?"

"I came to congratulate you!" I tell him.

"Huh? On what?" Joe asks.

"On your brilliant article!"

He screws his face up. "What you talking about, man? It was obviously Summer who wrote that."

I fix him with a stare. "Oh, you did a good job of making it *seem* like Summer wrote it. And I'm sure she was only too happy to provide a few quotes. But the actual article? You wrote that. And I would have fallen for it if it wasn't for the one thing which gave it away as being you."

Joe crosses his arms and says, "And what's that, *Velma*?"

I ignore his reference to *Scooby-Doo*, because I'm deadly serious about this, and none of it is funny. "You mentioned the pocket watches," I say. "That was something only Harvey and I talked about, and we decided to keep it a secret. It's just

Harvey slipped up once – in the gym, when he mentioned it in front of you."

Joe laughs and shakes his head. "Whatever, Alfie, you can't prove anything."

"He can't, but I can," says a voice behind me.

I spin around and there's Jas. She looks like she's already been up for three hours, composed and groomed as ever. She's brandishing a small pile of printed papers, like some kind of hot-shot lawyer.

"I smelled a rat too," Jas says. "That's why I contacted the website myself yesterday, posing as an editor from a *very* important magazine who just happened to love the prom article. And I asked if they could put me in touch with *Courtney Sinclair*."

Joe Chan's face suddenly drops, and Jas smiles smugly. "That's right, Joe," she says. "I guess they forwarded my email on because last night I got a reply from someone telling me they are Courtney Sinclair, writing under a pen name. They said they'd love to chat more about working with me – especially if I'm offering money." She shakes her head at Joe. "It was sent from your email address! You're Courtney Sinclair! Why did you do it?"

Joe's lip curls. For the first time, I see what he really feels when he looks at me – *disgust*. "I just didn't like what Harvey was doing," Joe says. "I thought it was wrong. I don't agree with all that LGBTQ+ stuff. That's my opinion, and I'm allowed to have it."

I glare at Joe because that's an argument I've heard a thousand times from ignorant bigots on social media. "What Harvey, or anyone else, chooses to do has no impact on your life whatsoever," I say. "Nor does who they are, or how they identify. Let people be. Let them do their thing. You don't like it? Then don't be part of it. But how dare you make their lives harder in the process? If that's your opinion, you can shove it where the sun don't shine, Joe – where it belongs, with the other shit."

"And, obviously, you're dumped," Jas tells him. "You prick."

With that, Jas and I flounce off. I'm breathless and shaking because I've never dared speak to anyone like Joe Chan like that before. I know horrible people lurk everywhere, but it's never nice to be reminded just how close they can be, and just what lengths some of them will go to in order to ruin your life.

"Well," Jas says, "I guess we're back to going to prom together?"

All I can think is, *I can't let those people win.* And before, maybe I would have let them. But now, I want to fight. Let's call it the Harvey Effect.

So, I shake my head and say, "Nah. Not that I don't love you, Jas, but I think you should ask Peter Popper. You said yourself he was fit, and Summer's dumped him after all."

"Okaaaay," Jas says. "And what about you?"

I turn to her, smile and say ...

CHAPTER 21

"I'm gonna go and get my boy."

CHAPTER 22

PROM DAY – 6 P.M.

I send Harvey numerous messages during the day, but he doesn't reply, although I can see he's read them. He doesn't even respond to the news that Joe was the one really behind the article. It's looking like Harvey's serious about not coming to prom, but I'm not going to give up that easily.

It's an hour until prom starts and I give myself a final glance in the mirror in my bedroom. It's the real deal this time – the full suit, shirt, bow tie … But without Harvey standing next to me like when we tried the pocket watches on, I don't feel the same sparkle and joy.

I've told Jas I'll meet her there, and if I go, I'll be going with Harvey or not at all. If I can't persuade him, if Harvey really doesn't want to come, then I don't want to go either. I won't be able to enjoy myself, knowing that his night has been ruined, and I don't want to spend my time with the people responsible for ruining it.

I spend what feels like half an hour standing outside Harvey's house, knocking at his door. I'm about to admit defeat when I glimpse a shadow moving in the hallway beyond the stained-glass panels. "Harvey?" I call out.

The figure moves closer. "I'm not coming," Harvey says.

"Can we just talk at least?" I ask.

There's a pause and then he opens the door. He's in his grey joggers, a white T-shirt and his hair is all messy. Harvey looks wrecked. I reckon he's about to tell me to go away, when he stops short, looks me up and down, and his face softens. "You look nice," he says.

"Nice enough to go to prom with?" I say hopefully.

He shakes his head. "Nice try. Come in, if you want."

Harvey's house is much bigger than mine. He leads me into a wide hallway and we take a right into a lounge with huge sofas around a fireplace. He indicates for me to sit on one and he takes the sofa opposite. He's keeping his distance and it feels like there's a full-on wall between us right now, not just a coffee table.

I know what it feels like. Two years ago, when I was working out who I was, I built walls too. I shut people out. I didn't want them talking about stuff that I didn't even know myself yet. It was for self-protection. So, I'm not going to try to break Harvey's walls down. But I am going to let him know that it's safe on the other side, if he wants to join me.

"Sometimes I think about how much easier life would be if it wasn't for other people," I say.

Harvey's staring down at the floor and doesn't reply.

"Like, would I have asked you to prom months ago if I hadn't worried about how much other people would roast me for it?" I continue.

Now he's looking at me.

I give him a smile and say, "I wonder a lot about all the things I might have done if we weren't conditioned to be so scared of what other people think."

"Yeah," Harvey agrees. "Everyone's so ready to take the piss, gossip and plaster your antics all over TikTok."

I nod.

"So, would you really have asked me to prom months ago?"

"Oh my god, Harvey, *yes*. But I mean, only in my wildest dreams. There's no way I'd normally have the guts."

"And yet you did ask me," Harvey says.

"Yeah, cause I made out like it was a joke. It's just that you happened to accept, which, by the way, made my entire freakin' year."

Harvey smiles, just briefly, then looks down again. He's a bit embarrassed, I think.

"Big questions are hard. Big answers are probably even harder," I say. "But everyone's got them, and everyone feels entitled to answers. Even when you don't have them, right?"

"Right," Harvey mumbles, not looking up.

"So, how about we make this a zone with no questions and answers? How about we don't try to define our feelings, pigeon-hole ourselves, or explain anything? How about we just live in the moment and enjoy it?"

Harvey looks up at me again. "You don't want to know ... anything?"

"Not a thing," I tell him.

"Not even ..."

"Nothing," I tell him again.

Harvey stares at me for a moment. "Huh," he says. Then he smiles. "Huh," he says again. And then he laughs. "Oh, wow," he chuckles.

I raise my eyebrows. Is that a good reaction?

Harvey releases a long breath. "I know you said 'no questions', but in case you're wondering, that feels good. Knowing there won't be questions and there doesn't have to be answers. That feels *really* good."

"I'm glad," I say.

"Also," Harvey continues, "how dare everyone else think I owe them those answers? Seriously, screw Joe and Summer and everyone else who's been judging me and chatting shit behind my back!"

I smile. Harvey's spark seems to be back.

"It makes me so angry," Harvey continues, jumping up and pacing about. "People's lives are their own business and they're allowed to tell you stuff when they're ready – not when someone else demands it!" He turns to me, a determined look on his face. "We're not gonna let them win. Gimme ten minutes," he says.

"What for?" I ask.

"So I can get ready," Harvey replies. "And by the way, you just asked a question. But that's OK. Because ... screw everyone. We're going to prom!"

CHAPTER 23

PROM DAY – 6.30 P.M.

Harvey calls me up to his bedroom exactly ten minutes later. When I finally see him, my breath catches. Sure, he's always handsome, but in his tux and bow tie he's jaw-droppingly *sexy*.

"What do you reckon?" Harvey asks. "Not too shabby?"

I swallow. My mouth is dry. I can't think what to say. He's so gorgeous I've forgotten words.

"Come here," he murmurs.

I walk up to him, shaking like jelly, because I'm not sure what's going to happen. He produces the pocket watches and I relax again. Harvey attaches one to my waistcoat, just like he did that day round at mine, then I do the same to him. We both turn and look at ourselves in the mirror and then he turns to me. Before I know it, his arms are around me and he's holding me tight, his face buried in my shoulder and mine in his.

And. We. Just. Breathe.

We. Just. Exist.

No questions.

No answers.

No doubts.

No fears.

No one else.

No judgement.

Just us.

Perfect.

CHAPTER 24

PROM DAY – 7.15 P.M.

By the time we get to school, everyone is already inside the main hall. If Harvey is nervous, he isn't showing it. I'm certainly not. Not with Harvey by my side. I feel free for the first time in forever.

We walk into the hall. It kills me to admit it, but Summer and the prom committee have done a stunning job with the decor. The ceiling has been covered in billowing drapes from which hang giant playing cards. There are large round tables with chairs in one half of the hall. They're covered in multi-coloured tablecloths and afternoon tea stands, on which sit sandwiches, sausage rolls and cakes. There are also mismatched cups and saucers at each place setting, and ridiculous teapots – one is shaped like an elephant with the trunk for a spout. I can also see bottles of punch on each table, with labels that read "Drink Me!" (Currently non-alcoholic, but it won't be for long.)

The other half of the hall has a dance floor made to look like a giant chessboard, complete with giant chess pieces. There are big soft toadstools scattered around the perimeter for people to sit on and the whole thing is bathed in purple and pink light. It's magical. And, despite everything, there *is* magic in the air tonight. The magic of *change*. I can feel it.

Harvey and I stroll a little further into the hall side by side. It's like time stops, the music stops, and everyone turns to look at us. In reality, I don't think any of those things happen, but sometimes you just zone in on the stuff that matters, right? And what matters right now is the people staring at us from across the hall: Summer Gray, Joe Chan and their assorted hangers-on.

Their eyes are boring into us.

They're waiting.

For their answers.

Are we together?

Is Harvey gay?

Is he bi?

And every other variation you can think of that'll be the subject of some delicious gossip.

Across the hall, I see Jas and Peter Popper, their faces welcoming, friendly and non-judgemental. That's the difference, see? Jas and Peter don't care about anything except the fact they're pleased we're here. They're the type of people you have to surround yourself with. The ones who love you just as you are, whoever you are.

Summer's face is stony and impossible to read. And then Joe Chan snakes his arm around her waist and he pulls her towards him. Summer makes eye contact with Harvey, then she suddenly pushes Joe Chan off her and screams, "Get off me, you homophobic creep!"

There's a collective gasp from all of Year Eleven, cause this is seriously unchartered territory and anything could happen now.

It's clear that Joe can't believe Summer just did that. He's just staring at her, a WTF? look on his face.

Summer walks towards us and I brace myself.

"I didn't know about the article," she says. "I didn't say any of that stuff – Joe made it all up. And I mean, *everything*." Summer turns to me. "I did try to warn you what some of the lads are like and how they think."

I nod, because, fair enough, she did, that time in the department store. But really? "You didn't say *any* of it?" I ask her.

"Alfie, do you seriously think I'd say something like 'It's Adam and Eve, not Adam and Steve'? Who do you think I am? Someone who pays for a blue tick on Twitter, or whatever the hell it's now called?" She sighs. "Oh, don't worry, I've already instructed lawyers. Joe won't get away with it." She nods at one of her lackeys (a girl called Kristel), who pulls out her phone and starts filming. "But that aside," Summer continues, doing a little hair flick for the benefit of the camera, "I suppose I have to admit I haven't behaved particularly well myself – even if you did both drive me to it. Just because I'm beautiful and popular doesn't mean I don't have feelings. I'm actually really deep? Like, I totally cry every time I watch *Toy Story 3*. I suppose I just didn't want to lose you, Harvey, because ... well, it's always been you and me, hasn't it? You were the Romeo to my Juliet, Prince Harry to my Meghan Markle, and—"

"Shrek to your donkey?" Kristel interrupts, seemingly lost in a romantic haze.

Summer scowls at Kristel. "First of all, shut up. Secondly, you'll need to cut that bit out – I'm not being compared to a *donkey*." She rolls her eyes, then turns her attention back to me and Harvey. "Having seen the extent of anti-LGBT hate in this school—" she glances at Joe, "—I'm launching a new social media channel to combat bigotry. I'll do this by getting brands to pay for me to travel around the world reporting on gay things."

"Gay things?" Harvey says, squinting at her.

"I dunno, like Pride in Brazil. Or a five-star trip to that Greek island called Lesbos where lesbians were invented."

My eyes nearly pop out at her ignorance. "*What?*" I say.

Summer ignores me and smiles at the camera. "I'm Summer Gray, and this is my channel: *Gray Goes Gay!*" She clears her throat. "Although I'm not actually gay myself. Just an ally. As long as there's money and likes involved." She smiles at me and Harvey. "Have a nice night, boys. You can go now."

Everyone watches Summer turn and disappear into the crowd.

Then everyone turns back to look at me and Harvey.

There's this weird silence. Like no one quite knows what to do now. And I get it, because everything feels upside down. Maybe that's appropriate since the prom theme is *Alice in Wonderland*.

Except, maybe, for the first time, everything is actually the right way up. It's just that none of us are used to it.

Harvey takes a breath.

And he reaches for my hand.

His fingers lace through mine.

And he squeezes.

Are we boyfriends?

Friends?

Or is this just a show of solidarity in the face of the haters?

I ignore the questions in my head because, right now, the answers don't matter anyway.

Tonight, we're just going to be.

Tonight, we're just going to live.

Why don't you try it sometime?

Our books are tested
for children and young people by
children and young people.

Thanks to everyone who consulted on
a manuscript for their time and effort in
helping us to make our books better
for our readers.